HOW THE MOONJAR WAS MADE

Created by Eulalie M. Scandiuzzi
Edited by Denny Blaine
Illustrated by James Drury

Special thanks to: Carlo Scandiuzzi, Nathalie Scandiuzzi, Eulalie B. Schneider,
Sarah Bergmann, Angela McNamara, Mary Ryan Karges, Tatum Kerr, Sue Larkin,
Marybeth Satterlee, Charlene Y. Stern, and Natalie Hernandez.

Printed in China

For Nathalie and Sebastien

HOW THE MOONJAR WAS MADE

Created by Eulalie M. Scandiuzzi   Illustrated by James Drury

This is Noom. Noom is a dreamer.

Noom dreams big dreams and little dreams and in-between dreams.

He dreams at school and at home and climbs trees just to dream.

This is Raj. Raj is a thinker.

She thinks about making rockets that will fly to the moon, and about the weather there, if she'll need her rain jacket, and who will be co-pilot.

So, Raj is a thinker

...and Noom is a dreamer.

One day Noom went to the schoolyard where Raj was sorting plain rocks from rocks with rings.

Noom said, " I collect rocks too! I collect flat skipping rocks, but the really flat ones are hard to find!"

Raj likes to collect rocks with circles on them.
Sometimes she puts her rocks in big high piles.

And sometimes she thinks about all the special places that she can save her rocks.

Noom likes to trade his skipping rocks for the perfect present or shoes that will make him jump high. He always has a few extra rocks in his pocket for special trades.

Noom couldn't help but notice Raj with all her rocks and Raj couldn't stop thinking about Noom with his special jumping shoes.

That night Noom dreamt that he had saved as many rocks as Raj.

And Raj sat up thinking about all the fun things Noom had spent his rocks on.

The next day at school Noom and Raj asked the teacher which was better, saving or spending?

"Well," said the teacher, "both are equally important! My mother had a jar for saving and one for spending and perhaps the most important was for sharing."

After school, Noom and Raj went for a walk and talked about what the teacher had said about sharing. They wondered who helped people who didn't have rocks or shoes or something special for trades.

Noom suggested they find some nice containers for their best rocks.
Raj agreed full-heartedly.

They found a candy box, but it wasn't big enough for all their rocks.

Then they found a tin camping cup, but it still wasn't big enough for all their rocks.

They looked and looked but the later it got the thirstier they got and the harder it was to find anything.

Raj asked Noom if he liked tea and honey. He said he loved tea and honey and milk and cookies!

Aha! Tea tins! perfect! One tin had Earl Grey written on it, the other had Jasmine printed on it, and the third was labeled Oolong.

Noom thought they should cover the tins to remind themselves which jar was for saving, which was for spending, and which was for sharing.

After a while, Noom said he was excited to save some rocks for a motor for his go-cart. Raj looked at Noom and asked him if he'd help her trade some of her rocks for a motor for her rocket ship.

They sat down with the new box they had made together.
Raj was dreaming and Noom was thinking.
Noom said he wanted to save some of his rocks to share with children who didn't have jumping shoes. Raj said she wanted to share her rocks with animals on the moon who wanted to learn the Moonsing language.

The next day they brought their invention to school to show their teacher and friends. Giovanni said "Wow! How did you make that?" and Spike said "that gives ME an idea!" The teacher added, "Very clever idea indeed- save, spend and share all in one!
Three cheers for Noom and Raj!"

YAAAAAYYY!!!! They were so happy, that Noom
spun Raj around and around and around!

And that was how the Moonjar was made.

Moonjar (moon-jar)
Moon: "To shoot for the moon"; to go after dreams and goals.
Jar: Following ancient custom where wishes or dreams
are written down and placed in a special jar for future celebration!
Moon + jar = MOONJAR!

To get your very own Moonjar, go to www.moonjar.com.